The Habit of Buenos Aires

The Habit of Buenos Aires

Lorraine Healy

THE PATRICIA BIBBY BOOK AWARD, 2009

TEBOT BACH • HUNTINGTON BEACH • CALIFORNIA • 2010

Cover photo: "Old One In La Boca" by Lorraine Healy, 2003
Design, layout by Melanie Matheson, Rolling Rhino Communications

ISBN 13:   978-1-893670-51-8
ISBN 10:   1-893670-51-1

Library of Congress Control Number: 2010925251

A Tebot Bach book

Tebot Bach, Welsh for little teapot, is A Nonprofit Public Benefit Corporation which sponsors workshops, forums, lectures, and publications. Tebot Bach books are distributed by Small Press Distribution, Armadillo and Ingram.

The Tebot Bach Mission: Advancing Literacy, Strengthening Community, and transforming life experiences with the power of poetry through readings, workshops, and publications.

This book is made possible by a grant from The San Diego Foundation Steven R. and Lera B. Smith Fund at the recommendation of Lera Smith.

www.tebotbach.org

para María

para Carito

para Papá

Yo quiero ser, llorando, el hortelano

"Elegía", Miguel Hernández

CONTENTS

INTRODUCTION

LORRAINE HEALY HAS DRAWN THE TITLE of her always powerful and consistently stunning collection of poems, *The Habit of Buenos Aires*, from an epigraph by Eavan Boland: "What I had lost/ was not land/ but the habit of land." Many of the poems in this collection echo the Peron years, and the long years of anguish—under the military junta—that held Argentina in their grip (Healy was born in Buenos Aires and lived there into her late twenties). This volume is both a personal record and a poetic autobiography fixed in time and place, and yet these poems gather to form a spiritual and political accounting as well. They also chart the cartography of a land slowly being lost to violence and lies and corruption; the poet, in the act of writing these poems, seeks to make her claim—a new claim, a poetic claim—on the land that was once her home. Muscular and immediate, these poems are resonant with superb details that allow, even at their darkest moments, an exceptional intimacy between the poet and her readers.

Lorraine Healy's poems include personal elegies for family members as well as more public reflections on cultural loss, yet the poems never resort to the abstractions of time or time's passage—they trust the particularity of their details and the clarity and force of their vignettes to convey both the character and the dimension of those losses the speaker sees and has experienced.

Lorraine Healy also weaves poems of first love and mature love through her arcs of narrative, and the humor and graciousness of these poems stand as a buoyant counterbalance to the darkness of some of the political poems. Equally compelling are those poems that unravel the Irish braid of Lorraine Healy's ancestry, as well as several fabulously evocative poems that trace her Italian lineage—all of which makes for a quite gloriously woven tapestry indeed.

Yet the ever-present context for all of Lorraine Healy's reflections remains the Buenos Aires of fact, of the past, and of her imagination. It is a province of interior nightmare tied to her childhood and young adulthood, one that needs exploration now that she is both the adult she is and the poet she has become. *The Habit of Buenes Aires* is a superb collection of poems, and in its pages Lorraine Healy has forged a truly remarkable debut.

—DAVID ST. JOHN

What I had lost
was not land
but the habit of land

Eavan Boland, *"Domestic Interior"*. *Part 8: After A Childhood*
Away From Ireland

la ciudad que nos sueña a todos

Octavio Paz, *"Hablo de la ciudad"*

I

the years of sorrow

The General's Hands

In the mid 1980's, General Perón's mausoleum in Buenos Aires was broken into, his coffin opened, and his hands cut off. His hands have never been found.

The ones that rappelled
into the small house of his death,
like medieval holy thieves
hunting for relics,
sawed off his hands neatly
at the wrist, however neatly
was possible after ten years
of green and purple putrefaction,
after the lullabies of maggots.
The dead general in all likelihood
did not flinch. The only job those hands had had
was to hold on to a rosary. Or
his curved saber, I can't remember.

But I remember this: a day
and an afternoon later,
stopped at the railroad tracks
a dozen smiling men
let themselves loose
amid the idling cars,
holding a little widget,
a coiled spring crowned
with a pair of tiny hands that moved
back and forth, back and forth,
just like the general
greeting the crowds
from his balcony at *Casa Rosada*.
He would call them "*¡Compañeros!*"
his companions, friends;
the crowd thundered back,
"*¡Mi general! ¡Mi general!*"

While waiting for the train, for the black
and yellow barrier to go up,
the cheerful men shoving

the little waving hands into our windshields,
for dos pesos, compañero,
you take the General's hands home
with you, "*¡Las manitos*
del General, dos pesos!
Las manitos del General,"
the General's little hands.

Eva

Blond of eternity, forever silk
and dust from Junín,
its scent of departing train platform.
What is there left to say about her?
Life short, shiv-edged,
a crown of voices under the balcony,
la Eva.

In our tired familial myth,
my doctor Grandpa injected her with penicillin
in this or that cubbyhole of Alvear Hospital,
"because she was always a *puta*" and she brought
the remnants of her gonorrhea, her syphilis.
We tugged our middle class behind us, its wounded
decency, the daily demijohns empty of wine,
replete of horror.

And more: Eva, my adolescent mother's
first cadaver, a girl dragged
to the lines in front of the weeping Congress
on that incomprehensible winter of '52—
to bid farewell to the fairy tale Eva, motionless,
wholly crystal, princess
condemned to sleep, perfect wax.

And for those who were not us, what?
For the ones who got her Christmas *pan dulce*, hard cider,
the brand-new bicycle, their first dignity,
for those with an intact devotion, Santa
Evita of the shanties and industrial suburbs,
a crass woman working cheap miracles.

If she had lived until wrinkles and fury,
if we had seen her in black by Paquito Jamandreu
with an armful of flowers withered with history,
her eyes hardening with the malice of cataracts. But no.

She left at the age of prophets.
To a heaven of guilt, the hell of memory,
the endless purgatory of having been Argentinean.
(And did you fuck her, Grandpa,
splayed on an examining-room table,
the future Spiritual Captain of the Nation?)

Eva of the poor, the General's sap,
fifteen year old of the railways always belonging to others.
Prodigal daughter of the provinces' misery,
Eva of the street market, of the slum, of the Bajo,
that stinking slope where mud meets brown river
which never had the silver it promised. Eva

with impossibly tight hair in a bun
on every billboard of the motherland.

March 24, 1976

I had just turned thirteen.

The dark early morning of March,
its first slim hooks of chill
snagging us all the way
to the bus stop. We sat
on the best row, the five-seater
in the back, amazed at our luck;
and looking out the window
the stillness
of the empty streets. Forsaken candy wrappers
and bus tickets suddenly aloft in wind,
then landing on the sidewalk, safe
for another day—there would be
no garbage run for nights. The school
deserted, *how come*
you not heard, Stefan,
the Polish janitor, asked
through the wrought iron bars.
Another empty bus home, our keys
surprising Mom. There was no school.
There'd been a coup.

There'd been a coup.

The Dirty War Dead

You were in somebody's address book,
you had a beard, you looked
like somebody else who was the one they wanted,
they transposed one of the digits in the number
of your street address, you had long
hair and were not a female,
you were not red but pink.
Maybe you did believe in Mao,
Karl Marx, el Che.

Sans license plates, the green Ford Falcons
with their three or four crewcuts in dark shades
descended on the city with the night.
By then, some things were like
breathing: curfew at eleven, two pieces
of ID in the inside pocket
of my school blazer; the shapeless fear.

You were tortured, raped, maimed, dropped
from an Army plane into the muddy waters
of the Río de la Plata, you were shot
and buried in a mass grave, you
were pregnant and spared until your babies
were born, then some officer took them,
killed you, reported your children as his own.

I was twelve, thirteen, fourteen,
agonized by oily hair and jeans
that never fit quite right, swimming
three miles a day, doing homework.
I didn't see them pick you up
and stuff you into the Falcon's trunk.
I was on the safe side of town.
I had been asleep for hours.

Plaza de Mayo, Thursday, 3.30pm

Crossing the avenue slowly
in knots of threes and fours,
they whip out the white embroidered
head scarves from battered bags,
tying them under the soft chins,
and move to the obelisk that celebrates
some freedom, where others wait
to peck their cheeks, ask after a troubled relative
or each other's rheumy legs in support hose.
They have begun their round of steps, marching
on cheap shapeless shoes.
Out of nowhere, there are placards in the hands
that had been washing lunch dishes
two hours ago. The faces on the placards
show the hairdos and long sideburns
that raged more than twenty years ago.

The city circles the Plaza with a flood
of traffic and a few weary cops.
The mothers' pace is nothing
like the passersbys'. Weighted down
by their Gustavos, their Pablos,
the Claudias, Julios and Elsitas,
the slews of María del Carmenes,
they move in cadences of pain and years
flayed raw by menopause and absence.
The hidden ones that still keep
eyes on them smirk there's fewer
every Thursday—age and the erosions
of grief removing them from view,
unsightly madwomen
who haven't learned about moving on.

A breath before rush hour
they unchain their arms, kerchiefs
and placards disappear,
they join the lines for the buses

and the underground, once again simply
women from the barrios come downtown,
returning home where the old man
has remembered to water the ferns
and start a pot of white rice for tonight.
Home to take a load off, watch the evening
news that never names them anymore,
the obstinate madwomen
who move on and on until they
catch up with themselves, around
the obelisk that celebrates some freedom,
corpseless, unsilent, on aching feet.

Where They Were

They were in Sweden, in Paris.
In Mexico City. In Venezuela.
The thirty thousand, the however
many had not answered
the latest roll call.

So said the general. The colonels.
Some lieutenants. Even the few
cadets of the Army School I knew.
Gone to Denmark. To Barcelona.
Zipping through Rome in little

scooters. Sending postcards. Asking
their poor mothers for more money.
Who were the mothers in the Plaza?
Covering up for the gone.
Making a wretched, wretched noise.

I went from thirteen to eighteen
eating the white sour bread of lie,
and the way we sang bland rock 'n roll
quieted the whispers, kept us
light-blue and innocent.

They were in Lima, crowding Madrid,
smoking *la frula* of Amsterdam,
on the long solitary walk of exile;
alive but skinless with nostalgia,
alive and breathing the rare foreign air.

So said the majors. And the beautiful,
immaculate Navy cadets on deck,
and the police. The news anchormen
tut-tutting the rumors, patting their gilded
hair. Were they homesick, the gone?

And we awoke and were so heavy
with the black-green years. So much mud
to go through, sifting for little things,
an earring, one of the wrist bones, a name.
We had been celibate for the motherland.

There was such a roar instead of singing.
The news came from abroad in empty envelopes.
The full things were the ditches where
the gone were entwined and known only
to themselves and each tangled other.

The cadets wore royal blue crossed
with red silk sashes. They could dance.
Nobody knew how we had come to own
so much hatred. Nobody knew. Nobody.
Nunca supimos nada.

Girl Begging on the B Subway

You whom I could not save
Listen to me
        "Dedication," by Czeslaw Milosz

Now, after the fire is done with her,
with kissing and licking her hands
and wrists into browning roses,
with tonguing her nose away, leaving
her face a pocked, misshapen moon,
she stands aloof, somewhat ancient,
the way some heroes return from Hell.
Up and down these subway trains,
she faces each and every one of us,
who are whole no matter what,
who can never be this broken,
this tightly scarred.
The eyes she bores with
are intact, firm and empty.
They send us
on a scurrying of desperation, a few
coins to conjure her out of sight,
on her way down the tunnel
she inhabits, her monstrous
innocence of grafts, the blameless
repellent skin. She carries off
the pile of brass centavos
on the scaly cup of her hand.

La Boca

From stray ochre hamlets
from Genoa to Calabria,
they sailed to this most South
of places, to the mouth
of a no-account river edging the city.

They built precarious, waiting
for news of soil,
throwing together corrugated tin
colored with myriad bits of paint
leftover from the ships.

While they waited,
the women strung the wash,
wiring window to window, hoping
the sun would find them there,
among the urban and the incomprehensible.

While they waited,
the men took to the river for its muddy catch,
to shipyards and docks, to *fare l'America*
on the hems of this place
where sunlight couldn't be counted on,
and faith was placed in rosemary
growing in three-legged flowerpots,
chipped red and green.

While they waited,
they let loose their joyful sibilants
and a dance of hands, into the oily river
and the city, into the fruit stands
of the street market, and farther even,
where the street corners
never flooded.

And this happened:
their voices married the new language,
changing it forever;
they got used
to the waiting and so they stayed, tied
to yellow and cobalt, their thirst
for land abated.

They cackled,
magenta and green laughter
mixed in with elbows and white sweat;
they aired their aprons and swept
the cobblestones, learned to love
thrushes and sparrows, grew gray

and faded, dozing on small stools
on the sidewalks, dreaming long
dreams of Tyrrhenian blue.

Las Kollas

Kolla women

Triangular, small chunks of the Andes
squatting on the sidewalk,
the women who came from Bolivia
offer their portable market on a canvas.
Years ago, all they sold
was tangerines. Now there is nothing
they don't sell:
peppers, sets of needles,
parsley, cheap underwear,
lemons and children's sneakers.
They weather exhaust
from traffic and news
of revolutions, the insolence of haggling,
blue-collared scorn. They add
boxes of strawberries in season.
Sometimes a young child who looks
like them hovers nearby, minding
a baby. With the manners
they brought from their highlands
they refuse to engage
in small talk. If short on change,
they'll offer a tiny head of garlic
for the coin they lack.

Dusk flies them
to invisible orchards,
mysteries hidden under
the stacks of wooden fruit boxes.
First light falls upon their hunched
silhouettes, grown to the chosen sidewalk
like the blades of grass
pushing between serrated tiles.

The Old Ones of Saavedra

They don't have much of anything,
but time? Ah… plenty of that.
So they can squander it like this,
supervising the fine
summer evening, commenting
on the immobile air as they sip
from wet cans of beer,
sitting on wicker stools
at this happy crossroads
of thresholds and sidewalk,
where the younger stroll
on the way to fluorescent pizzerias, malls.
The men in dignified pajama-
bottoms and cotton *camisetas*, the women
stirring the night with the half-moons
of their fans. The pots of angel hair soup
left to bubble alone inside, with only tin bowls
of white peaches to witness.
Outside, fireflies are keeping the old
people of Saavedra busy with delight.
Buenos Aires is all that is South
of them, all that is siren
and haste. The city
is everything that has forgotten them,
forgotten the pleasures of wicker stools
or the bliss of callused feet
in house slippers open to summer,
the happening of nothing,
the obstinate scent of jasmine,
Saavedra punctuated by dentureless laugh.

Twenty nine years later
March 24, 1976-2005

(un *kyrie* berreta)

i

It was the day we lost
the soul's weathervane.
Our throats filled up
with sulphur and benzene,
our breaths killed all geraniums.
It was without respect to the river,
it was then we dared
forget the simple decency of wolves.

Sometimes a south'easter tumbled over us,
the sky with its throat cut.
Sour, sour tangerines.
Everything took to being scarce, the air first.

We forgot to sigh in the afternoon.
We forgot to bless the ground.

We condemned our selves to not knowing
what to do with so much day.
To await the storm of hunger on our own,
which was still years and years away.

We can't write the full moon into a poem,
any poem, ever again.

ii

At 3.20 in the morning, it starts,
a slow-flapping funereal bird,
the official drone of the communiqué,
the Seal of the Republic floating
alone on the TV screen, rousing

martial music without end.
Everyone's black-and-white
TVs are off—Buenos Aires
sleeps.

iii

General Videla repeats before the foreign press:
"They are neither dead nor alive; they are
disappeared."

iv

And there was a before.
A time of random explosions
tolling around the city
like malignant bells.
An *us* and *them.* A generation
of clear-eyed idealists
marching up Córdoba Avenue
towards Utopia. Tear gas.
Twenty-something good kids
with sudden guns in their hands,
to build a socialist *patria.*
The beautiful idiot children
of middle classes who'd never seen
a furrow or the inside
of the assembly line
calling the exhausted peon "my brother."
Powered by red wine and dreams,
cigarrillos Particulares all night
and the hazel eyes of Che.
Their innocent hearts bled dry,
chaffed with solidarity.
The immense temptation
of their submachine guns,
the ones they quartered bomb by bomb,
with the irons, *los fierros,* of their compassion.

v

From the depths,
these our chasms, we who are
guilty of complacency and blindness:
a home-made, cheapo Kyrie
for the gone, the scattered, the ones
we could have been. Look
at the impeccable garments
we render, the ash
we pour on hair innocent of sweat;
forgive, forgive.

The country I flee from daily

It is the only tendriled
country in the world.
Its needy limbs reaching for miles
pulling me back into its despair.

It has so many little voices
announcing the annual revolutions,
the catastrophes of each month,
misery weekly.

Everything there needs me back:
the floods, the starving, the dark-souled.
To witness as the coffers
are covered with black velvet

and disappear.
To go behind the funeral procession
and wail. So many gone.

"Return, return!" plead the tiny
voices. "You'll have a place of honor
at the wakes; you'll have sweet foods."
But they don't even touch the silk robes
of belonging. This blood of longing.

The land's heartbreaking grasp,
its smother.
The dead keep quiet, but the soil
that barely covers them calls out.

But I am saved, I say.
And I am far.

At night the voices burrow
in my dreams and pluck
my broken heart strings.
They play dirges for the dead.
They cry all night.

II

kissing the cobblestones

My Mother's Faith

Before she goes to sleep
she covers us all
with her blanket of saints—
Gaetan for steady work,
Jude for the impossible,
Roche for infections,
Martin of Porres I forget why
except she and I like to sweep
and so does Martin, smile beaming
from his brown face on the prayer card,
hands holding a straw broom for eternity.
She calls on Our Ladies of Everywhere,
of every place the busy Mary
has ever been known to appear—
another woman stuck to a million chores
for a family as scattered
as the stars.

My mother knows reams of saints
to be, beatified obscure
souls, saints in training.
She loves them all,
with an unquestioning democracy
of belief, walking into
every darkened church
to gasp delighted
at the plaster figures staring blank
into the holy air,
greeting them like kin.

If saints can blush, these surely do,
pleased and embarrassed—
they can't help but bestow
miracles upon her, which she takes home,
these marvels soft and round like *gorriones*,
simple, uncomplicated miracles
she passes on to all of us,
who have forgotten how to pray.

End of November

This is a night I do not sleep,
spent listening to the breath in you
that starts to come from broken rocks,
from sudden flash flood.
Your dying becomes too big
for the house we live in,
for what we can hold with certainty.
As I drive behind the ambulance
that carries you—already gone from you,
from whom we knew—
your knowing dog howls from the yard.

With dawn, in the hospital, we enter
the territories of last. Last, murmured word,
greeting the ghost of your mother.
Last shape of you, contracting
into creeping cold, conquering
your random restlessness. Outside,
it never stops being Sunday morning.
There are thin coral clouds
and a scent of soily heat, of things
to come. The small future
of what a day involves, you remember.
And while I turn to tell you this,
your face has fled. As if you meant
to leave by turns, first went the heat,
then the soft male light of your expression,
its handsome shine. You linger
in the open mouth, your breath
coming in tiny see-through feathers.
And after one, so like the rest, your mouth
stays open and silent, a church door
after all have blessed themselves
and gone.

Jardín de Paz

I do not visit his louvered house,
where the family keeps pace
with life. Instead, I go
to his other house, a plain
slab of granite set in grass.
The rectangular shape of his sleep
sunk a little lower each time
as his body goes. It takes
a steeling of the sternum to kneel down
but then my hand finds its way
to his name, caressing the stone,
the last skin of my father's.
I tell it the news and call it Dad—my fingers
absent-minded in the grooves of the dates
when he was here and ours.

I make slow friends
with this quiet place, this corner
by the nameless red bush,
the tidy silence, the green
grids of those we lost.
Isn't it all a bit too circumspect
for you? I ask him. No one answers.
My father would have laughed.
But now? Has he acquired
the gravity of the dead?
And inch by inch the soil that covers him
compacts upon what's left,
rain bathing the helpless bones.

On the 16th Anniversary of María's death

This is how you are etched
into me: the scents
of *Magno* soap and the old-fashioned
gentility of *Maderas de Oriente,*
plain shoes with their wink of heel,
the way you piled on the straight
black wool skirts
when it was cold, your crown
of hair, a dandelion
ready to be blown.
How we cheated biology,
you and Mom and I,
she no less your child
for not having passed through you,
I no less your grandchild
for not sharing stray strands of DNA.
How fortunate we were in your wealth
of songs and tales, how you gave
of them, of everything, with such abandon.
I see your hands under the kitchen faucet
cleaning the mauve glove of a squid
I would not taste, not then,
not ever.
                    You came
from a lost world
where cows could cry,
with a river of laundresses
and you a child who loved soap.
I have a 2 by 2 inch picture
of you at 30, one leg
in front of the other to slim
your slim hips, the wavy garçon
hair of 1935.
It all got trampled by the boots
of Franco's soldiers
after you were already gone

into the country of 1,000 revolutions,
south of everything, for good.
Here's what you'd never see again:
your mother, your bossy sister Matilde,
the river, the village, all
of Spain for that matter,
the Northern Hemisphere.

Your firm footsteps,
your horror of self-pity,
white-haired titan of a woman
in bright-colored sweaters
and a narrow wool skirt,
panty-hosed until the hospital,
brave as a demi-goddess
and, like any of them, strung with light.
Unkillable, like a weed, until the cancer
but even so the *brisca* game with death
on your terms, with your deck,
cards on the bed and in the hands
I still manicured maniacally in ICU.
How beautiful were you, really? Who
can say? To me, beyond the sun and stars,
the one lap to sit on, while leaning out
to watch the frightening world.

The camellia that I bought one year ago today—
brought home and planted
later to discover
it carried your name—
has the first two blooms cracking open, crimson
so like your lipstick
and the full planets of your nails.

Crushes

Because you had pups' eyes
and an endearing

interminable lankiness
that went so well with

the thick straight hair or
because you were hunky

and homely, possessor
of an irresistible smile;

because I don't know
your wives or your bald spots

because I don't get to know
the stained silk of your failures

and remember you sixteen
absolutely perfect in the way

that your stubble was
perfect as it was scarce

and far between
in the way that your kissing

was perfect as it was
peckful and new;

because on odd nights
you come in droves

to crowd my dreams
and you fill up train wagons

going nowhere
still looking like you did

in 1978 but I know it's now
for you show up wearing

the smart suits of a success
you didn't think about then

when you smiled but didn't
fall for me or smiled

and kissed me a grand
total of three times;

or you smiled on your way
to wherever the gorgeous

were meant to gather;
because I wish you well

and wish you true
happiness if you still believe

it possible   because
of you—the thought of all of you—

who were my complete idea
of bliss for a time

because something of this rainy
weather after forty might

speak to you
of the grateful embarrassment

you still bring.

Getting It Right

After the first collisions of teeth, after
the disappointment of it, after he
asked around and somebody told
him "tongue, man" and he told me
in a fast whisper during school break;
after a few attempts to get
our noses tilted just so and lips
opened warily and then somehow
a gap that was just right and then
we had it, there it was,
the sheer melting of it,
the drip of delight as we
got it all together,
perfect and forever, this galloped breathing,
this red etching of his once-
a-week shave against my cheek,
oh we could have gone like this for hours, days,
oh weeks, the game of tongue
on tongue, the sudden spurts
of plain devouring, the magnetic
field we had created and kept
unbreaking, back for more,
back for more, pearl after pearl
after pearl in a long necklace,
this jewel
of a first kiss.

Your Mother's Hands

I remember it as the one good summer,
how many times we tried loving in the water
because that was my fantasy and you complied—
and no matter how hot the day or us
for each other, how slow you slipped my suit
down from the shoulders, how we took to it
like fighting lions—the water won
and turned us colder and colder
until we spilled out on the sun-white stones,
teeth chattering, a little angry that we couldn't make it
like a soft-core porn movie we had never watched,
how it never lived up to the films in our heads
and next time we would try the shower
and slide on tile and soap foam.

This was after we had learned the initial dance,
after your innocent, comely cock had stopped hurting
as it traveled in; yes, all was well, and you loved that I
could cook and satisfy at least some of your hungers.
In your truck, above its diesel music, we sang
along with Mercedes Sosa, "Las manos de mi madre,"
and both thought about your mother's hands
resolutely still in the year-long house of her death.
It was the one good summer we had, one out of three,
the future sweet and hefty, a new fruit we hadn't tried.

The hands that so mirrored your mother's
just as the song said, como pájaros en el aire,
birds alighting on my darkened skin,
testing the limits of my drowsy nap,
fingering the brim of my misguided happiness
again and again, its overflowing.
Does it matter that fall came and linden
and jasmine folded onto themselves and I lost
the power to beguile you? Can we count
kissing under the Southern Cross, call it something
to save? Your mother's hands have turned

to ashen paper and you, hair thinned,
sore elbow keeping you awake at night,
do you remember we glistened with blue water,
the sheen of that summer upon us?
How splendid, our faith in the hunger,
how radiant, our failure to come.

The Parallel Universe

—is where I say yes to you
the sun-drenched morning when I
turn 26 after the night
with moist roots into each other,
after you made me stare
at my breasts in the mirror
and there they were
my two strangers

—is where I trick you into
child after child after child
whom you don't want to give
the long brown of your sadness.
But this is where I blind you
because *I* want them—
swimming question marks that stretch
and vein me, orbing me away
from you at last

—is where we puzzle over them,
big-eyed enigmas so
unlike our fantasies, so real
playing in a bathtub where
the water gets colder and darker.
What we do: you towel them dry,
I comb their wet seal-like hair.

The parallel universe
is where you decide I have
burdened you enough and I turn
in bed and keep my hunger to myself
and we leave each other stranded
on a road invisible to everyone.
And you hiss that you shouldn't
have asked me. And I spit
on your November sun.

III

the emigrant Irish

The Cilleens

In Ireland, fields where stillborn or unbaptised babies were buried

They sleep in unconsecrated soil,
already in a limbo of fields—
in their tiny decomposing
bodies, unsanctioned
and returning to the innocence of humus.

In their mothers' hearts,
a little stone for each of them,
etched with a ghostly name—
she would have been a Bridget,
he could have been a Padraig—
and a date distorted by the pain.

Born blue, born lost, stillborn,
small clots of flesh buried by neighbors
in cardboard boxes, dug shallow in the Cilleens.

They sleep now in this mother of a field
that deemed them innocent, holy enough.

A Song for Mary Egan   (1865-1903)

This is the flashflood of her blood
following endlessly after the stillborn babe,
the tenth, her last,
the one she has to run after
leaving the other six live ones behind,
this the one she needs to hold close forever
in the silent lullaby of rest.
She is no good now, you see,
she's worn her insides down
to thread, three gone already
and this wee thing born and lost today,
cloaked in its mother's gown of blood,
unstoppable,
running with it into the March light,
this Patrick's Day, into the feast
of morning, oh the red of it
on the dewy green of spring,
the breeze of their passing, together
almost, the mother after the child
like a sweet game of chase.
This is the one she can't live
without, her other six left
to God's thrifty mercy, this
is the one that leads her out
and away and beyond rain
and beyond sorrow into another field
of forgetting and a peace
like madness, that new
and full of flight.

Lament for Six Voices

Thomas weeps by the windrows
in the field. Sean's voice strangles
on the daily blade of asthma.
Patrick will be silent for years,
until the day he's found by the sweet lyre
of booze. Mary is five and Honor
three and what they sing
is the lilting song of not knowing
how very gone you are, Mary.
Michael, asleep in a crib,
will have no memories of you.

Your husband is roaming the roads
hunting for a woman
who'll take him, take the lot of them,
for a house and a few
rocky acres—for the chance
of some babes of her own.

She will sweep out your ghost
from the three rooms, she will
tell your children no stories. She'll have
no song. She will feed your man
from her hard bread, he will give her
five daughters and silence.

The living have to make do.
They pay their dues, heartbreak and all,
wake up and hum the prayers by rote,
those that help bring on the dawn.

The Road To Tulsk

Co. Roscommon, 1845

in front
of the stolid yellow stone house
where my great-great-grandfather
stood one morning a hundred
and sixty two years ago.
The morning he said the road
to Tulsk was a giant black
snake creeping eerily,
Mayo, Donegal, and Connemara
emptying off their peasants
starved in their unnourished step,
black snake undulating past his front door
for weeks, for months,
the ragged, the poisoned, the dazed
with no sanctuary except
in moving, an unholy,
saintless procession, hopeless
but in the walking.

Caught in metaphor, the good man.
Haunted by dark reptiles
forever sliding through the field of his sleep,

long past the road to Tulsk
becoming the road again,
and the ditches
forgot the contracted weightlessness
of the famished dead.

When James Kelly gathered his
and as many
as he thought the land could keep,
and kept them.

Great-grandchild of the Famine

What I know of the man
will barely fill a stanza: he
had a beautiful voice, he had
Burnside whiskers, he married late.
In 1847, he was not done
with being a child.

Bent over my kitchen sink,
a stainless steel peeler
in the hand that arthritis like his
will deform, I look at
the potato's oblong brownness.
This buoy of starch denied to millions
by years of blight.

How does the grace of survival
work? Who gets chosen?
What are the sounds of night
in a land where most everyone
is dying with blackened mouths
stewed in fungus and saliva?

The ones that could, fled.
Even the banshee must have jumped
aboard a coffin ship,
worn out from wailing,
sick of the stench.
The ones that stayed and lived
were saved by the forethought
of an apple tree or skinny chicks in a coop.
The three year old kept going by a stash of— what?
What sort of crumbs?

One hundred and fifty years
is nothing. Every morning demands
the choice between butter or jam—never

both for a great-grandchild of the Famine.
I have inherited all the confusions
that garnish food
but not a single recipe.
This straight line sails from him to me.
And I am whole,
forever starved for stories.

Need and the Grocery List

My grandmother wrote grocery lists in tinfoil
paper saved from the inside of Via Appia

menthol cigarette packs, and she wrote tiny
and lovely, a few things so very

needed so there would be room
for much Catholic denial. Her father

a Famine child, his longevity carried
like a heavy, undeserved cloak,

who stopped singing sea shanties across the fields
when his eldest son died of TB. One hundred

and sixty acres of grief, and hunger still fresh,
sown deep into the windrows. Short lists

of needs for Molly, then. On ironed scraps of shine,
an eternal inkpen fat on those fingers

so inexplicably angled, that we asked about
with the breathless cruelty of children—

eluding Mother's dismayed warning eyes.
But Molly was a chuckler, and kind, and remote

to us in her language of penance and distant home.
A few, few things were needed, thought out,

spread through the days. It was up to our souls
to remember, to save squares of tinfoil paper,

the way Molly did,
at the foot of that cross, undistracted,

always choosing less, calling it enough.
We learned how tightly cramped it was

inside desire, how gorgeous
the braid of want and guilt we would wear

forevermore because there once
was a vastness of starving across the island

still lodged in our cells, that dry burr.

Family Tree

Within the folds of faith
they found a space to worship
soil and its belongings,
and in the songs of birthplace—
Menlo, Rathcroghan, Ballinagare—
a cause as old as humankind.
Mother-orphaned boy he was,
coming from near the sea,
tubercular, dark-haired,
bringing behind him
the very broken weather and silence
sewn to the fabric
of his sooty black suit.
A profile in cameo, a long
trail of handsome brothers,
she grew up next to hay
and ruins, and a half-invented
lineage of shepherd kings.
Legend has it they fell in love
while dancing—from jigs
one step to running guns.
In the nightmare of the 20's
he was marked for the noose,
a terrorist in love with her
and with the tunes that memory plays—
Menlo, Rathcroghan, Ballinagare.
They left on different boats
to the very ends of the world,
which they would people furiously.
How did they come
to detest each other's sights,
to refuse to eat from
one same set of spoons?
The past, their constellation
of locked doors.
I come from them. I have

her hair, his bony hands
on a different hoe, that wildness.
On rainy nights like this,
my bloodstream echoes
Menlo, Rathcroghan, Ballinagare.

IV
return to Buenos Aires

To Go To Buenos Aires

There was always too much of Lvov...
(Adam Zagajewski)

There was always too much of Buenos Aires, a weight
on the shoulders like a full load of wet cobblestones,

it was endless how the violet blue of the jacarandá,
it is now or never at the corner where the bus door

yes, no, opens, won't, the random brown of human indifference
and who begs at one threshold but sleeps across the next;

there was one trolley car down Paraguay Street, a silver Leyland, #31,
forever the thin blue line of gas in winter,

which will sputter, which will die, and the ride home on the #132,
so much cement flowering in the neighborhood, its Hassidic

men in bunches like black grapes, armies of old ladies
who were mean to cockroaches, who rolled shopping handcarts

with milk in green bottles and six eggs wrapped in newsprint;
there were stops at the railway crossings to let a slow-witted train

move out to what was not Buenos Aires and therefore
did not, could not, exist, call it impatient

honking from the motorists done with waiting and radio
commentary because it will be better tomorrow, how can't it

not, this abundance of Buenos Aires flooding the yellow air,
Autumn again and olive-green tanks overtake the Plaza,

our yearly revolution but what can't this city survive,
cancel the melancholy and what is there left, marble

statues and cemetery vaults for our unforgiven beloveds.
And always more, more Buenos Aires, stretched

to the arbors growing on courtyards where the non-city
starts, those places of domestic poultry and clotheslines.

Snuck under the secret trapdoors of Buenos Aires, such burlap,
metal tacks, stashes of broken bricks, as many as I

have memories, potholes filled with rain water and see
how the foliage reflects on them, how easy

to believe it is all benign and as blissful
as the air of March when it bends into April, that slope

into the arc of Buenos Aires where it is now and forever
hailing petals and the streets spew lime.

Barrio del Once

We look at the world once, in childhood
The rest is memory
Louise Glück, "Nostos"

I am once again surrounded
by flocks of the Orthodox
Jews of my childhood,
dreamy-eyes, black-frocked
benevolence, crows of unexpected
silence. Only they remain quiet
in the neighborhood where I grew up,
a babel of bolts of cloth
and a merchant's sense of itself,
with coins clinking in all pockets.
A place too busy for beauty,
buses running down its veins.

Coming home from school at dusk
I got off one of those buses
desperate with the urge to pee.
Untroubled by the wealth of pharmacies,
one per corner and filled
with half-limbs and white enameled
horror, I felt content
with this, my place on earth,
the young women in their inexplicable wigs,
the soot of air, the policeman
perched on his pulpit above it all,
this was the time before traffic lights,
holding the twin rivers of the avenue
quite still, as the trickle
of Larrea street moved
while it still had a chance.

Buenos Aires changes around it
and the neighborhood stays put,
caught in its business of cheap,

the fake and the rapidly fading,
polyester by the yard, this place
of no silks.
It stays the same and turns ancient,
growing a kosher butcher per block,
every cobblestone rooted in commerce,
small vans lining the streets like trees.
The Pole next to the Armenian
and, next to him, the Ukrainian's store.
I knew their spices waving in the air,
the boys with long side curls
and the long sigh that came
with Friday night, the silence
of all Saturdays, and on Sundays
the day awoke with Our Lady
of Carmel's bells, calling
the few to Mass.

Belated Elegy for Padre Kohlm

Cassocked since dawn,
his red Germanic hair raised an unconscious
flag of fear in us,
his school-year flock at Santa Julia's
which sat concretely on the corner,
a neighborhood church replete
of unpaid debts to beauty.
And he the parish priest,
who stepped out of cold air
as if coming down from the stained
glass, martial and vertical,
a line of perfect tiny black buttons
bisecting the body he'd as soon have forgotten.
Eight year olds like well-behaved
ants on the pews, we waited
to be called, boys to the open door
of the latticed wood confessional,
within woeful range of the old men's flash
of slap on their 3rd grade faces;
girls to the side sliding window
where we wouldn't tempt
their priestly, antediluvian eyes.
Padre Kohlm clasped pink hand
over pink hand with a clap
that was dead easy to mock,
and he had questions
on our years of sins.
Had we helped with chores?
Mmmm... No, Padre. Unholy language?
several times a day,
and on he went ruefully, intent
on civilizing, that other salvation;
while we lied through our new
half-grown front teeth.

And on a spring November Saturday,
Buenos Aires lit blue in jacarandas,

we filed, in eyelet white
like midget brides, in dry-cleaned
school uniforms with silk and satin bows
on their left arms, girls and boys
clutching mother-of-pearl missal
between prayerful hands, down
the aisle to the altar
where Padre Kohlm with tamed red curls
approved of our docility
and shone exalted, as if
wholly made of saintly patent leather.

What happened, so much later, to Kohlm
and his battalion of naphthalene-smelling old priests:
they pruned in the sun of their courtyard
at Santa Julia's, toppling over dry,
milk-eyed.
Or were they shoed away by backstabbing
congregations wanting guitars and good news
and long-haired priests out of a *telenovela?*
Or did Padre Kohlm lead them into a winter
night, nothing more to be heard from them,
the flock of well-intentioned magpies flying skyward.

Easter Eggs

Soon after Carnival,
indecently mocking Lent,
the bakery's windows sprouted
round dark treasures
nestled in fake hay:
eggs of coarse chocolate
covered with stiff pastel-sugar swans,
all wrapped
in noisy cellophane.

And sometimes,
in poorer years,
they languished for weeks,
the teal and yellow swans fading
with the autumn sun,
shrinking daily,
until the arrival of Corpus
Christi and winter swept them
from view,
replaced by plain flutes
of golden bread of the day.

Saint Rita

Santa Rita, lo que te da, te quita
(Saint Rita, what she giveth, she taketh away)
(popular Spanish saying)

i

In Cascia, perched yellow
on an eastern Umbrian hill,

inside a crystal coffin, like a fairy tale
princess, dead asleep, is Rita,

patron saint of the impossibles;
one dead foot impossibly flipped
back, the other laid on the cushion.

She is turning brown with time,
fully dead and incorruptible, fully
sainted, freak show but not

for the kneeling faithful around
the wrought-iron grates, the crystal cases

containing babies' bibs and pacifiers,
those conceived in surprise and prayer,

or hammered tin in the shape of limbs,
of hearts, the tin *milagros* of the healed,

incense and spent wax hanging
in the blue air of her church.

ii

Seventy miles west, a waxen Clara of Assisi
sleeps in another crystal coffin,
plump and unreal.

In a different crypt, my mother
thinks she sees Francis' remains
in what looks to me like

a disheveled bird's nest,
which she insists is his skull.

Umbria is dotted with saints
and cypress and these impossible
golden towns perched on hills.

We go from Benedict to Scholastica
to Valentine, into the crypts that smell
of mold and wet rock,

where the polychrome of the Madonnas' feet
has been kissed away by years
of love and madly devoted hands touching.

We walk up the hot stone *vias*—indolent sun,
muted birds, the borrowed death of *siesta*—my mother carries
the invisible cross of her depression

to yet another church.

iii

On a baked July keeling towards
August, I saw so many of the pious,
their eyes celestial, blessed and woeful,
among them my mother, palm
against palm the way she learned in childhood;
and all were on their knees,
silently asking a browned corpse encased in glass
for some impossibility.

This, believe me, is how it goes:
the tiny corpse, its raisin face impassive,
has the ear of God, and God's favor.
She only *looks* immobile, peaceful.

Saints are those who spend their eternities
at work for others, relaying prayer
to God's symmetrical feet.
God is so busy. The saints insist:
"Hear me, hear me... This one's deserving"
In this place of air there are no
impossibilities. Rita tugs the Lord's sleeve.

iv

Rita who pined to be a nun
and was married off to the town watchman
who beat her up faithfully

Rita who wanted peace and gave birth
to twin boys thirsty with vengeance;
Rita and her three violent men who died young

freeing her for the convent, where she finally
dove into her love for Christ, who sent her
a ring of bleeding around her head,

his phantom thorns to Rita,
circular rubies of ache,
the Christ's terrible loving.

Five hundred and fifty years of this,
turning like a prune, a pit-less date
inside the black habit

in the perfect house of her crystal peace
in the royal blue of her hideous church
on the warm stone of this Umbrian hill

amid the lame and the wheelchaired,
amid the steady pilgrimage of the broken,
all of us watching Rita's long sleep,

a tiara of bloody flowers around her head,
the obliterated men she was given to love,
Rita at peace with her flipped foot

on a velvet cushion, what to ask
of her silence, what impossible prayer
dies in my chest while my mother kneels on the steps,

my mother mentally unfolding the long list
of her intentions, asking Rita to hold
the hearts of those my mother loves

who happen to be suffering from loneliness,
bad marriages, sterility or are under
the desperate hex of something,

lets call it life, all of which
she lays at Rita's dead unsymmetrical feet
with the docile certainty of her faith.

And around us the old women in house dresses
clic-clicking rosary beads, the spent tallow
of candles as yellow as Cascia, smoking a little

thread of thin black smoke, will it dull
the demented blue of the walls, I wonder;
will it sneak into the crystal case

and brown Rita's papyrus skin, how
would that be for impossible and what's a saint
to do with so much asking?

v

Outside, flapping in the scorching July breeze,
a parking ticket trapped by a windshield wiper
on our rental, punishment for stumbling

into the wrong parcheggio after the green
switchbacks up this hill. My mother says,
see? Rita's already taking away.

On a Visit Home, I Ask My Mother Whereabouts in Emilia-Romagna—Italy—Her Grandparents Came From

I
She says call Uncle Julio,
he'll be the one to know,
but Julio's mind is wrapped
around what to do about the family
vault, in the cemetery of the forever
middle-classed; who to will
the scrolled iron key to—once he is gone.
No one wants to deal with the small catastrophes
of hail the size of grapefruits smashing
the little windows through which
our dead peek and watch
the polluted seasons of Buenos Aires.

Moreover, Julio adds,
the 99-year lease has expired
and the cemetery wants money or
its little house back—crumbling cement,
the unbearable mustiness, three flights
of stairs down to rooms furnished
with the hard beds where the coffins sleep.

II
Uncle Julio who looks like Uncle
Enrique who looks like Roque and Rafael
who looks like Aunt Ani who mirrors Mom,
all nosed with eagle beaks, hair straighter
than an old Roman road, not one
as wrinkled as Great Uncle Emilio but
give them time. All meant to last long,
clinging to their teeth, eyes buried
under plies of crow's feet.

III
Questions about emptying the vault:

what to do about, say, Antonio and Esther,
whose own two daughters are dead, how to track
down elusive cousins to present them
with reductions to ash, small urns
carrying a kilo of bone brittle.

Or Emilio himself, passed away at a thousand or so,
obdurately single, who of us will take
wrinkled Great Uncle Emilio under
our reluctant wing, burn him, find him
an unmoveable place of rest. Who will claim

Great Aunt Assunta, married
for exactly one day before she left
that never described sinner—the day-old
husband—and went home to pray,
and pray, and pray, her room
under the perpetual fog
of candles she burned to the saints.

IV
When Julio says "Ravenna!"
I believe it's another Italian curse, but

no, he says, "Ravenna!" and
I see the place where Dante

died of the wide ache of exile;
somehow I know this is not right,

not Ravenna where the old *abuelos*
came from, too lofty for the kind

of amiable peasants who'd become
grocers in the New World, who,

at night, made children joyously,
as if following an ancient recipe.

"Ravenna..." says Julio, cupolas
covered in gilded mosaics of flat Christs,

flat Madonnas, Ravenna, says Julio
walking through the skinny roads

that separate the houses of the dead,
where it is moving day for our departed:

how will I leave this place with three urns
under my arm, grandparents, infant uncle,

will I have to take a taxi or can I hop
on the # 44 bus and walk the rest of the way,

me and them, our little family procession,
will I keep singing "Ravenna, Ravenna..."

as a dirge to them, especially the little one,
the boy my Mother was conceived to replace.

This garage sale of relatives, we dour
and uncomfortable, live ones, who resent

the siblings who sent us here to collect
rotten coffins and metal containers

of who we don't remember, the ones
that came from a mythic Ravenna,

the ones who now have to be placed
somewhere as we leave Uncle Julio

to gather all the lost, unclaimed muertos
who had once come to dinner and would tell

Julio about the lime-white dawns of Ravenna,
the honest truth of what never happened. Ever.

Easter then, Easter now

The man buried in Buenos Aires today
stopped a coup in its olive green tracks—
it was Easter 1987, at the coup's head
one soldier with a Bedouin name
and a face made of cliffs and ridges

and you and I watched it all on TV,
the pageant of it, the threat of tanks
and no mercy in that first Autumn wind,
an unfolding to doleful narration,
a Passion of sorts right on the screen

but I was too distracted by how thoroughly I loved you,
burned with what you refused to offer, and weeping
was my daily office, with Easter opening the door
to another winter of your eyes and their elsewheres—
when the man buried today

came and went, came and went endlessly
while the soldiers' faces were lathered in shoe-black,
ready to take the tired whore of Buenos Aires
and fuck us all good and dead
in the spirit of the season

but he stopped it— the dead president just buried
this Easter—who that April came and went,
came and went so endlessly
as he preached the unpromiseable,
as he tattered his soul in the firesale that was Sunday,

came out into the Pink House's balcony to say
"The house is in order. Happy Easter!"
to the crowd we hadn't joined but should have,
this man they buried today in Buenos Aires
under a shower of linden leaves.

It still confuses me: the death, the resurrection,
how deranged in love with you I was,
the man who stopped the colonels
buried today, carried on soldiers' shoulders—
and you are smoke and sweetness, church bells, history.

What My Father Sees, If He's Ghosting

Barefoot, he swims laps of air,
not a blessed pocket to his name.
Aloft on thermals, he sees the dogs

lose color to the years, me
middleaging, and he nods but refrains
from wisecracks— what has become
of his mindlessness?

He approves of the garden, epic
and obdurate, he notes its careful
wintering. Wholeheartedly he approves
of my love, who senses him clung to nimbus.

A breeze hooks my face up,
as if snagged by a flute-length of song.
What a perspective, with that much
above and over.
                    The future of lined-up
afternoons in an attendance log,
which he checks with the ghost
of his MontBlanc pen, also passed.

He has bet big on my happiness—
where he perches, weightless
and princely, well past the hour of green.

The kite of him taunts these red alders.
Lord, he is joyful around the edges,
all those distant stars he swallows.

A Poem Before We Face The Business of Death

On Mondays across eight thousand miles,
you and I hash the weathers of the week,
sweet saucy lipsticked and storied, you tiny mother,
who carry the daily load of your panic with peaceful hands.
I take up the refusal of your cooking,
I notch each laugh
of yours on an invisible totem pole.
This is about looking at you and bowing with every breath.
This is about returning every one of your terrors, unwanted.
About your hatred of genealogy, when
you and I make one such thorough line.
You third girl, undesired, born after
the irreplaceable dead boy, the prodigal
who never came back from pneumonia and silence.
Your green eyes are turning the skyblue
that trumpets cataracts. The way, when I visit,
I pick up the small lint of things
that you no longer see. This is about your right
to cry to dubbed reruns of *La Familia Ingalls,*
the things that are sacred to you,
sacred to God, the male one,
and his winged minions. This is about you and me
living like newborns, small animals
who have known captivity and escaped. Over the phone
I hear the police sirens of our Buenos Aires
and I tell you about the robins crowding my woods.
I shall inherit every age spot of your arms,
all the yellow that time brands on your skin,
the silver peeking stubborn through your blonde hair,
you who leave such treasure. Open handed you go
to kiss the beggars and buy from the poorest peddler.
Despite the miles, I go behind you, touching
my forehead to the cobblestones you tread.

NOTES

"Where They Were" is for Anne Marie Macari, who pushed for it.

"Twenty Nine Years Later": General Videla's verbatim statement to the foreign press is from an Op-Ed piece by Osvaldo Bayer, *Página 12*, Buenos Aires, 24 March, 2005. The line "los fierros de la compasión" is from Juan Gelman's poem "¿A Quién?" in *País que fue, será*.

"End of November" and "Jardín de Paz" are for my father, Brian M. Healy, 1936-2000.

cilleens: a small patch of unconsecrated ground in the area of the parish, where babies that died unbaptised or were still born were buried, usually in board boxes. Sometimes a little marker was put on the spot.

"The Cilleens," "A Song for Mary Egan," "Lament for Six Voices," "Great-grandchild of the Famine," "The Road to Tulsk": with thanks to my cousins Mary Healy Nackley, Mary Kelly Knipfer, John S. Kelly, and the late Kathy Kelly for sharing the family stories.

"Song for Mary Egan" and "Lament for Six Voices" are for and about my great-grandmother Mary Egan Healy (1865-1903), and the children she left orphaned, including her second, Sean, my grandfather.

"The Road to Tulsk" is for my great-great-grandfather, James Kelly. "Great-Grandchild of the Famine" is for James' son, Michael Kelly, my great-grandfather, 1844-1929. "Need and the Grocery List" is for their child and grandchild, my grandmother Molly Kelly Healy, 1900-1990.

"Your Mother's Hands" was inspired by the poem "Burn" by L.J. Sysko. Thanks, Les.

"Easter Then, Easter Now" alludes to the government of Raúl Alfonsín (1927 –2009), the first democratically-elected president of Argentina following the military dictatorship. Alfonsín ruled from 1983 to 1989, peacefully deflected an attempted coup by military officers in April of 1987.

ACKNOWLEDGMENTS

Grateful acknowledgement is made to the editors of the following journals, where some of these poems were published (sometimes in slightly different form):
The Raven Chronicles, Switched-on Gutemberg (on line), Seattle Review, Kimera, Celtic Bardsong, The Southern Cross (Argentina), PoetsWest, Rio Grande Review, Calyx, Poems & Plays, Margin Journal of Magic Realism, Anthropology & Humanism, Carpetas de Luz y Poesía, Sling & Rock. Some of these poems appeared in my chapbook *The Farthest South*, winner of the New American Press contest of 2003.

"Plaza de Mayo…"won 1st prize at the Hackney Awards, 2001
"My Mother's Faith" received an honorable mention from Kimera magazine, 2002.
"Plaza de Mayo…" and ""The Dirty War Dead" were performed live at the *Viva la Word* festival in Portland, OR, in 2003.
"Las Kollas" received an International Merit Award from the Atlanta Review, 2003
"The General's Hands" won 2nd Place at the Society of Anthropology & Humanism Award, 2005
"End of November" was nominated for a Pushcart Prize in 2004 (under the title "An Artifact of Light").
"Saint Rita" and "Your Mother's Hands" were finalists for the Paumanok Prize, 2006
"Belated Elegy For Padre Kohlm" was a finalist for The Virginia Brundehlbuhler Award from Sling & Rock magazine, 2007
"A Poem Before We Face the Business of Death" received the 1st Prize at the 2007 Lois Cranston Award from Calyx Journal.
"Saint Rita" was a finalist for the Rita Dove Prize, Salem College, in 2008.
"To Go To Buenos Aires" received an honorable mention at the Ann Stanford Poetry Contest of Southern California Review, 2008.
"Jardín de Paz" appears in the anthology Beloved on the Earth: 150 Poems of Grief and Gratitude by Holy Cow! Press.
"Need and The Grocery List" appears in the Fall 2009 issue of Crab Orchard Review.
"On A Vist Home…" was a semi-finalist for the Pablo Neruda Prize and appears in the October 2009 issue of Nimrod.

A generous fellowship from the Fishtrap Writing Community in 2008 allowed me to unleash a huge amount of new work, triggered by the wonderful Paulann Petersen.

also: *gracias, gracias, gracias…*
to my mentors Paula McLain, Anne Marie Macari, Joan Larkin, Alicia Ostriker, and Michael Waters, *über*-mentors Maxine Kumin and Gerald Stern, and the entire faculty of the MFA Program at New England College, 2004-2006;
to the poets whose generous support helped me get a green card on the sole grounds of my poetry: Laure-Anne Bosselaar, Maxine Kumin, Thomas Lux, Anne Marie Macari, Alicia Ostriker, Gerald Stern, and Eleanor Wilner;
to my friends and first readers, who read these poems tirelessly: Lana Ayers, Marian Blue, Misha Cahnmann, Janlori Goldman, "Shoe" Shoemaker, Leslie Sysko;
to my aunt Mary B. Healy, *sine qua non;*
to the entire Healy Clan of Buenos Aires, for their patient, unwavering support; to my parents; to María Riopedre and Carolina Díaz Martínez, under whose light I walk forever;
and, never least, to the providers of gladness: Dianne MoonDancer, Gus, and Mendieta.

This book is set in 10 pt Giovanni book.